THE WORLD'S TOP TEN

MOUNTAIN RANGES

Neil Morris

ILLUSTRATED BY VANESSA CARD

RSVP

RAINTREE
Steck-Vaughn
PUBLISHERS
The Steck-Vaughn Company

Austin, Texas

Words in **bold** are explained in the glossary
on pages 30–31.

Text copyright © Neil Morris 1997
Illustrations copyright © Vanessa Card 1997
© Copyright 1997 Steck-Vaughn Company this edition

Published by Raintree Steck-Vaughn Publishers, an imprint of
Steck-Vaughn Company

Editors: Claire Edwards, Helene Resky
Designer: Dawn Apperley
Picture researchers: Juliet Duff, Diana Morris
Consultant: Elizabeth M. Lewis

Picture acknowledgements: Robert Harding Picture Library:
10 bottom, 25 top. FLPA: 22 bottom W. Wisniewski.
Mountain Camera: 5 bottom, 9 bottom, 12 bottom, 28 top all
John Cleare, 16 bottom and 17 top Colin Monteath.
NHPA: 15 ANT, 23 top Stephen Krasemann, 26 bottom Karl
Switak, 29 bottom John Shaw. Russia and the Republics Photo
Library: 28 bottom. Still Pictures: 8 bottom Mark Edwards, 18
bottom Bios/Julien Frebet, 20 bottom Bios/ Thierry Thomas, 21
top Bios /Alain Compost, 24 bottom Foto Natura/ James Philip
Nelson, 27 top Bios/Alain Compost. Tony Stone Images: 5 top
Colin Prior. TRIP: 11 bottom, 13 top, 29 top M. Jellife, Zefa: 19 top.

Library of Congress Cataloging-in-Publication Data
Morris, Neil.
    Mountain ranges / Neil Morris: : illustrated by Vanessa
Card.
      p.   cm. — (The world's top ten)
    Includes index.
    Summary: Introduces the ten major mountain ranges of the
world including the Andes, Himalayas, Rocky Mountains, and
Tien Shan and describes their formation, length, height, plant
and animal life, and human inhabitants.
    ISBN 0-8172-4339-9
    1. Mountains — Juvenile literature. [1. Mountains.]
I. Card, Vanessa, ill. II. Title. III. Series.
GB512.M66 1996
910'.02143 — dc20
                                         96-4091
                                       CIP AC

Printed in Hong Kong
Bound in the United States
1 2 3 4 5 6 7 8 9 0   00 99 98 97 96

Contents

What Is a Mountain Range?

A mountain range is a group of mountains that are side by side. Their peaks are separate, but their lower slopes join to form one piece of high land. When two or more mountain ranges are linked together, this is called a mountain chain. The longest and highest mountain ranges in the world, such as the Andes, Rocky Mountains, and Himalayas, are sometimes called mountain systems.

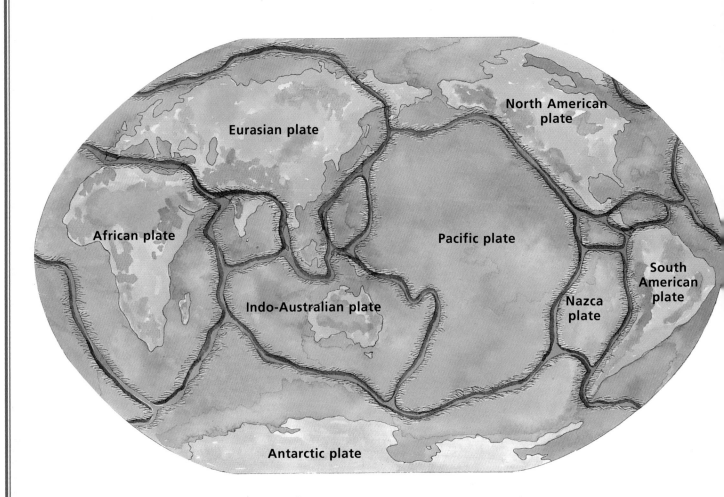

Eurasian plate

North American plate

African plate

Pacific plate

South American plate

Indo-Australian plate

Nazca plate

Antarctic plate

How mountain ranges form

The Earth's surface is made up of an outer layer of rocks, called its **crust**. The crust is cracked into huge pieces that fit together like a giant jigsaw puzzle. These pieces are called **plates.** The plates move against each other, sometimes causing earthquakes, and their edges buckle and crack. Although the plates move only a few inches each year, they press against each other enough over millions of years to crush the rocks into huge mountain ranges.

New and old ranges

The three longest mountain ranges in the world — the Andes, the Rocky Mountains and the Himalayas — are near plate edges and are still being pushed higher. At the edges of the plates, the Earth's crust is weak. Sometimes **molten** rock from inside the Earth bursts through to form a volcano.

The Great Dividing Range, the Transantarctic Mountains, the Brazilian Coastal Range, and the Tien Shan are much older ranges and are now farther from plate edges. They are lower because rain, wind, and ice have **eroded** them over millions of years.

The longest mountain ranges

In this book we take a look at the ten longest mountain ranges in the world. We see how similar and how different they are from each other and get to know the people and animals who live there.

The world's highest mountain, Mount Everest, lies among the snow-covered peaks of the Himalayas. The Himalayas are the third longest mountain range in the world.

The Dolomites are part of the Alps, which formed 10 to 25 million years ago. The mountains have been worn away by the weather into very steep, rocky peaks.

The Longest Mountain Ranges

This map shows the ten longest mountain ranges in the world. The Andes, Aleutian, and New Guinea ranges are part of the Ring of Fire, a huge circle of volcanic mountains around the Pacific Ocean.

Some of the longest mountain ranges are on the ocean floor. Sometimes just their valleys are underwater, but their **peaks** form chains of islands. The Sumatra–Java and Aleutian ranges are like this. One day mountain ranges that are now beneath the ocean may surface to form new land.

The World's Top Ten Mountain Ranges

1	Andes	4,500 mi
2	Rocky Mountains	3,000 mi
3	Himalayas	2,400 mi
4	Great Dividing Range	2,250 mi
5	Transantarctic Mountains	2,200 mi
6	Brazilian Coastal Range	1,900 mi
7	Sumatra–Java Range	1,800 mi
8	Aleutian Range	1,650 mi
9	Tien Shan	1,400 mi
10	New Guinea Range	1,250 mi

Aleutian Range

Rocky Mountains

NORTH AMERICA

ATLANTIC OCEAN

SOUTH AMERICA

Brazilian Coastal Range

Andes

PACIFIC OCEAN

Transantarctic Mountains

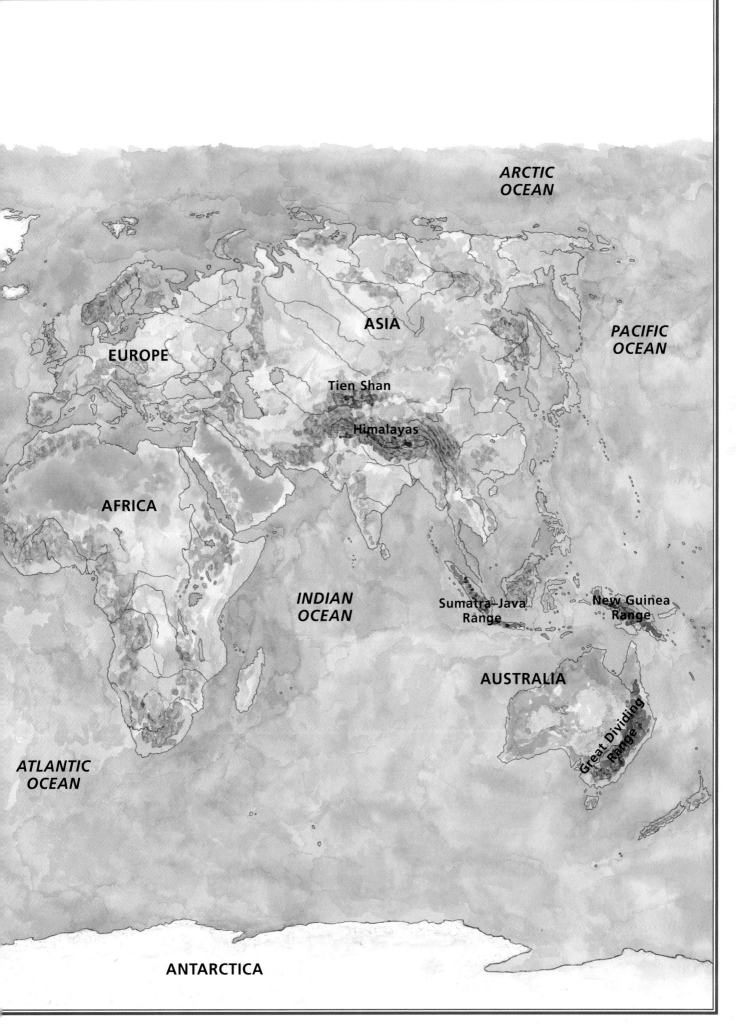

The Andes

The Andes are the longest mountain system in the world, stretching down the west coast of South America. The mountains form part of seven countries: Venezuela, Colombia, Ecuador, Peru, Bolivia, Argentina, and Chile.

Many kinds of land

Many mountain ranges make up the Andes. The highest peak of all, Aconcagua, is in Argentina. It rises to 22,836 feet (6,960 m). There are many kinds of land in the long Andes region. These include thick forests, **fertile** farmlands, and high, empty **plains**. There are big modern cities and small villages, where people have lived the same way for hundreds of years.

La Paz, in Bolivia, is the highest capital city in the world. It lies 12,001 feet (3,658 m) high in the Andes. About one million people live there.

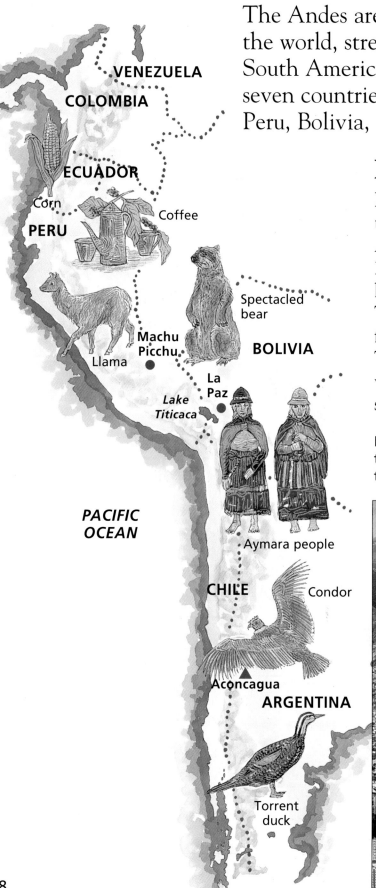

VENEZUELA

COLOMBIA

ECUADOR

Corn

Coffee

PERU

Llama

Machu Picchu

Spectacled bear

BOLIVIA

La Paz

Lake Titicaca

Aymara people

PACIFIC OCEAN

CHILE

Condor

Aconcagua

ARGENTINA

Torrent duck

FACTS

LENGTH 4,500 miles (7,200 km)

HIGHEST POINT Aconcagua, Argentina, 22,836 feet (6,960 m)

LOCATION Western South America

Native peoples

Before the Spanish **conquest** of South America, the Incas and many other native peoples lived in the Andes. When the Spanish arrived in the sixteenth century, they sent their own people to rule the area and destroyed the Inca Empire. In 1911 an old Inca town called Machu Picchu was discovered high up in the Andes of Peru.

Today Spanish is spoken in all the Andean countries. Many people are **mestizos**, which means people of mixed native and Spanish ancestors. Quechua, the language of the Incas, is still spoken by millions of Andeans in Bolivia, Ecuador, and Peru.

High lakes

Lake Titicaca is high in the Andes, between Bolivia and Peru. It is fed by 25 rivers and is the largest lake in South America. It is also the highest lake in the world, at 12,500 feet (3,810 m) above sea level. The Aymara live on the shores of the lake. They are farmers and fishers.

Farther south, in Bolivia and Chile, there are many large **salt lakes**. Some are completely dry and white, while others are gray or green. One lake is colored red by the unusual plants that live in it.

The ruins of the Inca town of Machu Picchu sit about 1,970 feet (600 m) above the Urubamba River. A royal palace and a temple lie among the ruins.

9

The Rocky Mountains

The Rocky Mountains, also called the Rockies, stretch down the western side of North America. This great mountain range is almost 3,110 miles (5,000 km) long, running all the way from northwest Canada to the southwestern United States. It is the second longest mountain range on Earth and is part of an even larger system called the western Cordillera.

FACTS

LENGTH   3,000 miles (4,800 km)

HIGHEST POINT   Mount Elbert, Colorado, 14,422 feet (4,399 m)

LOCATION   Western North America: the United States and Canada

Athabasca Glacier moves slowly down from the Columbia Icefield, high in the Canadian Rockies. Athabasca River flows from the foot of the glacier.

Glaciers and ice fields

The northern end of the Rocky Mountains begins in the Yukon Territory of Canada. Farther south, the mountains run along the border between the two Canadian provinces of British Columbia and Alberta. Here **glaciers** and rivers of melted ice move down the high valleys. A huge **ice field** is on top of Mount Columbia. Its melting waters feed ice-cold lakes and form rivers that flow into three different oceans: the Arctic, the Pacific, and the Atlantic.

National parks

There are two famous national parks where the Rocky Mountains cross the border between Canada and the United States. Together the Canadian Waterton Lakes and the American Glacier national parks form a large protected area known as the International Peace Park. This is the territory of black bears and grizzlies, moose and mule deer, and mountain lions and bighorn sheep. Mountain lions have been found on mountains over 13,120 feet (4,000 m) high.

Rocky peaks, called the Maroon Bells, tower over Maroon Lake, near Aspen. In the winter, when the mountains are covered in snow, this part of the Rocky Mountains is very popular for skiing.

Gold and silver

The Rocky Mountains are rich in **minerals**. There are large amounts of gold, silver, lead, **zinc**, copper, and **tungsten**. In 1859 there was a **gold rush** in the Colorado Rockies. Wagons rolled in. At first, people did not find much gold. Many wagons rolled east again. But soon gold and silver were discovered, and some people made their fortune. Today the snowcapped Colorado Rockies are more famous for their popular ski resorts, such as Vail and Aspen.

The Himalayas

The Himalayas are the world's highest mountain range. They stretch across the border between India and Tibet, through Bhutan and Nepal to northern Pakistan. They continue west as the Karakoram Range and the Hindu Kush into Afghanistan. This great mountain system is just over half the length of the Andes.

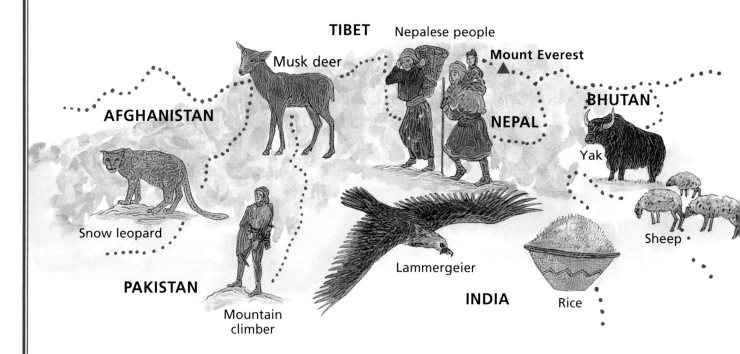

TIBET

Nepalese people

Musk deer

Mount Everest

AFGHANISTAN

BHUTAN

NEPAL

Yak

Snow leopard

Lammergeier

PAKISTAN

INDIA

Sheep

Mountain climber

Rice

Climbers walk toward a camp, which is over 19,685 feet (6,000 m) up Mount Everest.

On top of the world

The ten highest mountains in the world are all in the Himalayas. This includes the highest peak of all, Mount Everest, which lies on the border between Nepal and Tibet. To the people of Tibet, the mountain is known as Chomolungma, or "goddess-mother."

Mountain climbers did not reach the top of Mount Everest until 1953. **Satellite surveys** measured Mount Everest at 29,028 feet (8,863 m).

FACTS

LENGTH 2,400 miles (3,800 km)

HIGHEST POINT Mount Everest,
  Nepal/Tibet, 29,028 feet (8,848 m)

LOCATION Southern Asia

"Home of snow"

Himalaya means "home of snow" in the old Indian language of Sanskrit. The mountain peaks are all above the **snow line**, which begins at about 14,760 feet (4,500 m). This is 3,280 feet (1,000 m) above the **tree line**.

Two small kingdoms, Nepal and Bhutan, are in the Himalayas. Both countries have warm, wet lower slopes that can be used for farming. Higher up, the Sherpa people of Nepal and the Bhote, or Drukpa, of Bhutan grow rice, barley, and other crops.

Oxen pull a farmer's plow on the high slopes of Nepal. In the distance are the snowy peaks of Annapurna, one of the world's highest mountains.

Mountain animals

Some Himalayan mountain people live by herding large hairy oxen called yaks, as well as sheep and goats. A few yaks still live wild at heights of up to 19,685 feet (6,000 m), but so many have been hunted that they have almost died out. The powerful snow leopard hunts wild goats, called **ibex**, and small musk deer. The leopard has thick fur to keep warm, but in heavy snow and very cold weather it moves down into the valleys to find food. The Himalayan black bear lives in forests on the lower slopes, sleeping through the cold winter in caves or holes in trees.

The Great Dividing Range

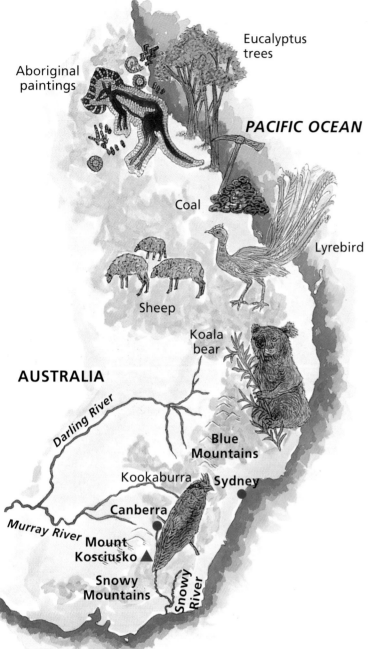

- Eucalyptus trees
- Aboriginal paintings
- **PACIFIC OCEAN**
- Coal
- Lyrebird
- Sheep
- Koala bear
- **AUSTRALIA**
- Darling River
- Blue Mountains
- Kookaburra
- Sydney
- Canberra
- Murray River
- Mount Kosciusko ▲
- Snowy Mountains
- Snowy River

Australia has only one long mountain range. The Great Dividing Range stretches from the north to the south of Australia. Although most of its mountains are lower than 4,920 feet (1,500 m), this mountain range is the fourth longest in the world.

Dividing the country

The Great Dividing Range got its name because it divides the east coast of Australia from the rest of the country. The distance from the range to the Pacific coast varies from 18 miles (30 km) to more than 185 miles (300 km). Europeans settled near the Pacific Ocean, where the land is fertile and the weather is good. The mountains separated them from the **outback** and desert areas.

At the north end of the mountain range, in Carnarvon National Park, there are Aboriginal rock and cave paintings. Aborigines, the original people of Australia, may have lived in these hills 19,000 years ago.

The Blue Mountains

The **foothills** of the Blue Mountains begin just 40 miles (65 km) from Sydney, the city with the most people. The mountains are about 3,610 feet (1,100 m) high, but there are deep valleys and canyons, where people like to walk and climb.

From a distance, the mountains often have a blue color, giving them their name. This blue appearance is caused by an oil given off by the **eucalyptus** trees that grow there.

FACTS

LENGTH   2,250 miles (3,600 km)

HIGHEST POINT   Mount Kosciusko, 7,310 feet (2,230 m)

LOCATION   Eastern Australia, across the states of Queensland, New South Wales, and Victoria

These sandstone rocks in the Blue Mountains are called the Three Sisters. Trees grow on the sides of the steep slopes.

The Snowy Mountains

In the south of Australia, where it is cooler, some of the Great Dividing Range peaks are snowcapped. There are ski lodges in the Snowy Mountains, not far from the mountain range's highest peak, Mount Kosciusko. There are several national parks in this area and an important **hydroelectric** plant. The Snowy River has been dammed. The water falls hundreds of feet, driving **generators** to make electricity for Canberra, Australia's capital city. Huge tunnels take water through the mountains to nearby farms.

This dam, in Kosciusko National Park, forms part of the Snowy Mountains hydroelectric plant. It's easy to see why the mountains were given their name.

15

The Transantarctic Mountains

A large sheet of ice covers Antarctica, the coldest **continent** on Earth. The South Pole is in Antarctica, which is divided in two by a range of mountains 2,200 miles (3,500 km) long. Antarctica is the world's highest continent, with half its area more than 6,560 feet (2,000 m) above sea level.

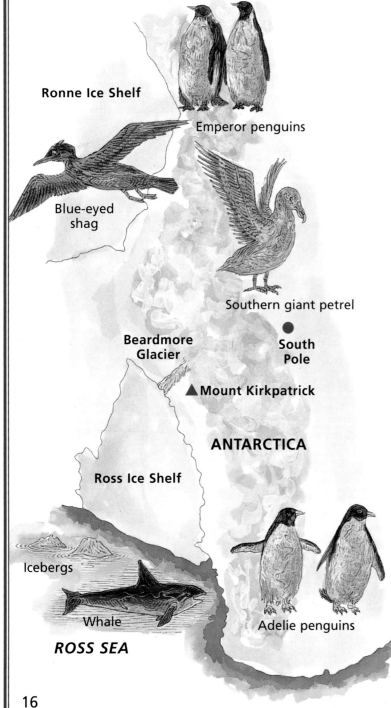

Ronne Ice Shelf

Emperor penguins

Blue-eyed shag

Southern giant petrel

Beardmore Glacier

South Pole

▲ Mount Kirkpatrick

ANTARCTICA

Ross Ice Shelf

Icebergs

Whale

Adelie penguins

ROSS SEA

Cold wilderness

Antarctica is very cold and windy. In some areas the average temperature over a whole year is as low as -72°F (-58°C). Winds can reach up to 200 miles per hour (320 kph), which is three times the speed of a **violent storm** in other parts of the world. In places the **ice sheet** is almost 3 miles (5 km) thick.

The rocks of some of the taller peaks of the Transantarctic Mountains stand out above the ice. This is unusual, because in most ranges it is the highest peaks that are covered with snow.

Many high areas of the Transantarctic range have rocky peaks and dry valleys, such as these in the Prince Albert Mountains.

High mountains overlook a flat layer of thick ice. This ice shelf forms the coast of the Ross Sea.

Glaciers and icebergs

There are many huge glaciers in the Transantarctic Mountains. The longest of them, the Beardmore Glacier, flows into a huge ocean of ice at the foot of the mountains. This is called the Ross Ice Shelf. Gigantic chunks of ice break off from the edge of the **ice shelf**, becoming **icebergs** that float away to sea.

FACTS

LENGTH   2,200 miles (3,500 km)

HIGHEST POINT   Mount Kirkpatrick, 14,855 feet (4,528 m)

LOCATION   Antarctica, from Victoria Land to the Weddell Sea

The mountains, glaciers, cold, and wind made the journey to the South Pole very difficult for explorers. In 1911 Robert Scott and four others climbed the Beardmore Glacier to reach the high Antarctic **plateau** and finally the South Pole. There they found a Norwegian flag: Roald Amundsen's team had beaten them to it. Scott and his men all died on their way back to base.

Changing climate

Scientists now think that the Earth's climate is becoming warmer. There are many signs of this happening in Antarctica. The two main types of flowering plant are spreading, and glaciers are beginning to move faster and melt more quickly. More icebergs are breaking away from the ice shelf, too. The weight of the ice on the land presses down, so if the ice melts, the land will begin to rise. The Transantarctic Mountains may then become even higher than they are now.

The Brazilian Coastal Range

The Brazilian Coastal Range stretches for 1,900 miles (3,000 km) close to the Atlantic coast of Brazil. The highest peak is Pico da Bandeira, which rises to 9,505 feet (2,897 m). This mountain is in the south of Brazil, not far from Rio de Janeiro.

BRAZIL

Diamonds

Anteater

Gold

Tupi

Carnival

Pico da Bandeira ▲
Rio de Janeiro

São Paulo

Great Escarpment

Coral snake

ATLANTIC
OCEAN

Armadillo

World's oldest rocks

The Brazilian Coastal Range forms the edge of a plateau that stretches toward the middle of Brazil. In this area are some of the oldest rocks on Earth. Scientists have discovered that some of the rocks date back to when the Earth was forming, at least 4.6 billion years ago. Since then, the mountains have been worn away by rain and wind, or **weathering**. Weathering has smoothed the mountains so that the land is mainly low and rounded.

Coffee plants grow well in the highlands, and there are many large plantations. Brazil is the world's biggest producer of coffee.

Living on the coast

The Tupi peoples lived in the forests of eastern Brazil long before Europeans arrived. Then, 500 years ago, an explorer named Pedro Alvares Cabral claimed Brazil for Portugal. At first, the range of highlands kept the new settlers from moving west. They stayed on the strip of low land that runs along the Atlantic coast. Today, most Brazilians still live between the coast and the mountains. Huge cities have grown up, including São Paulo and Rio de Janeiro. About 15 million people live in São Paulo, the biggest city in South America.

FACTS

LENGTH   1,900 miles (3,000 km)

HIGHEST POINT   Pico da Bandeira, 9,505 feet (2,897 m)

LOCATION   Eastern Brazil, near the Atlantic coast

Mountain riches

To the north of Rio de Janeiro, a series of mountain blocks rises like steps. South of Rio, the edge of the mountain range is steeper and higher, forming a wall. This steep edge is known as the Great Escarpment. When **settlers** made their way across the Great Escarpment and into the mountains, they found gold, diamonds, and other precious stones. The mountains are still mined for **iron ore**, **manganese**, and **quartz**.

Hundreds of years ago, settlers rushed to the Brazilian mountains in search of gold. Today, gold is still mined in the area.

The Sumatra–Java Range

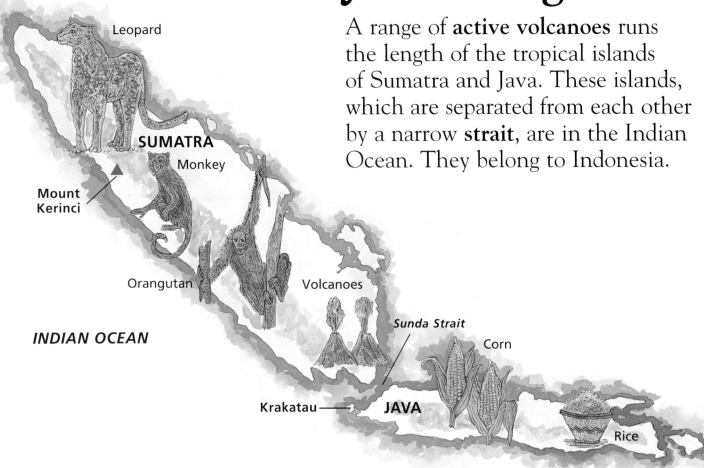

Leopard

SUMATRA

Monkey

Mount Kerinci

Orangutan

Volcanoes

INDIAN OCEAN

Sunda Strait

Corn

Krakatau — **JAVA**

Rice

A range of **active volcanoes** runs the length of the tropical islands of Sumatra and Java. These islands, which are separated from each other by a narrow **strait**, are in the Indian Ocean. They belong to Indonesia.

A fisherman's cabin on Lake Kerinci. The lake is in a valley near Mount Kerinci, the range's highest point.

The Sunda shelf

The islands of Sumatra and Java are really the tops of mountains. They are on the southern edge of the Earth's Eurasian plate. This area is called the Sunda shelf. Just south of the islands, where the Sunda shelf meets the Indo-Australian plate, is the Java Trench. Here the seabed falls to 25,344 feet (7,725 m) below sea level. When the two plates moved, a string of volcanoes was created that runs along the islands.

Anak Krakatau throws out lava as it erupts. This active volcano is now an island.

A volcano erupts

In 1883 the volcano Krakatau, in the Sunda Strait, **erupted**. The explosion destroyed two-thirds of the island and was heard 3,100 miles (5,000 km) away. The seabed moved, causing a series of giant ocean waves called **tsunamis**. When these 130-foot (40-m) waves hit the shores of Sumatra and Java, villages were destroyed, and more than 36,000 people were killed. In 1927 a new volcanic island appeared. It is called Anak Krakatau, or Child of Krakatau, and it has erupted often in recent years.

FACTS

LENGTH   1,800 miles (2,900 km)

HIGHEST POINT   Mount Kerinci, Sumatra, 12,467 feet (3,800 m)

LOCATION   Sumatra and Java, Indonesia, in the Indian Ocean

Active volcanoes

There are about 540 active volcanoes in the world, and 23 of these are on Java. In this century there have been at least 18 eruptions on the island. But more people live on Java than on the other Indonesian islands. One reason for this is that the island's volcanic ash is good for the soil. Rice, corn, and many other crops grow well in Java's volcanic soil and support the large number of people living there.

The Aleutian Range

The Aleutian Range, the world's eighth longest mountain range, stretches out as a **peninsula** and then a string of islands from the northwest tip of North America. The Aleutian Range is part of Alaska, the largest state. The Aleutian Islands, part of the mountain range, separate the Pacific Ocean from the Bering Sea.

Aleut

Mount Katmai

Puffin

Arctic tern

BERING SEA

Unimak Island

Fish

Seal

Shishaldin Volcano

PACIFIC OCEAN

Adak Island

Whale

Alaska Peninsula

A group of mountain ranges form a huge curve around Alaska's Pacific coast. First there are the Coast Mountains, then the Alaska Range, which is about 650 miles (1,046 km) long. Finally the Aleutian Range runs along the Alaska Peninsula. The peninsula's most famous peak, Mount Katmai, collapsed when a volcano erupted with terrible force in 1912. The eruption created the Valley of Ten Thousand Smokes, which years later was still giving off steam and volcanic gases.

Today the Valley of Ten Thousand Smokes looks like an empty desert, surrounded by snowcapped volcanoes.

22

An inlet on Adak Island, 620 miles (1,000 km) from the tip of the Alaska Peninsula. This remote island rises to a height of 3,224 feet (1,196 m).

Foggy islands

The Aleutian Range continues from the tip of the Alaska Peninsula as the Aleutian Islands, a chain of 150 islands. The islands are the tops of volcanic mountains, and their lower slopes are covered by the ocean. The highest peak, measured from sea level, is on the largest island, Unimak.

The climate on these islands and in their mountains is cool, wet, and foggy. The fog happens when warm air from the Pacific Ocean meets cold air coming from the Bering Sea.

Aleut people

The first people to live on the Aleutian Islands were relatives of the Inuit who crossed from the Alaskan mainland about 4,000 years ago. The Aleuts hunted for whales, seals, and sea otters from their kayaks. They caught fish with spears and fishhooks. Aleut families lived in homes dug into the ground and covered with grass, animal skins, and earth. Today there are only a few thousand Aleuts left. Some run fishing boats and others work in fish **canneries**.

FACTS

LENGTH 1,650 miles (2,600 km)

HIGHEST POINT Shishaldin Volcano, Unimak Island, 9,373 feet (2,857 m)

LOCATION Alaska Peninsula and Aleutian Islands, between the northwest Pacific Ocean and the Bering Sea

The Tien Shan

In Central Asia, the Tien Shan range forms a border between Kyrgyzstan and its neighbor, China. Kyrgyzstan was part of the former Soviet Union and became an independent country in 1991.

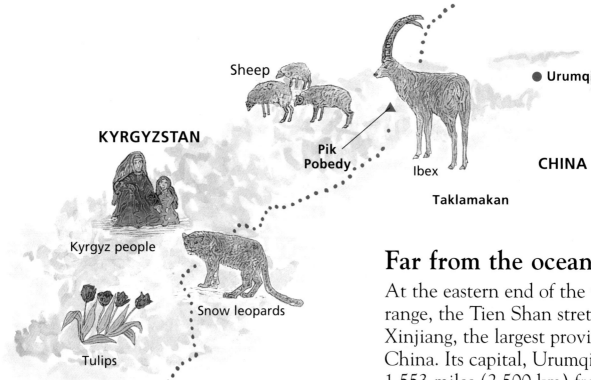

Far from the ocean

At the eastern end of the mountain range, the Tien Shan stretches into Xinjiang, the largest province in China. Its capital, Urumqi, is 1,553 miles (2,500 km) from the coast. This is farther from the ocean than anywhere else in the world. Just south of the Tien Shan is the Taklamakan desert. The desert is surrounded by mountains and is so far inland that it hardly ever rains.

There is a story that Tamerlane, a fourteenth-century Mongol chief, told his soldiers to put a stone in a pile as they crossed the Tien Shan. After the battle, each soldier took back a stone, so Tamerlane knew how many soldiers he had lost.

The Tien Shan peaks can be seen from this green valley in eastern Kyrgyzstan.

Kyrgyz people traditionally keep camels for milk and transportation. These people are crossing a plateau near the Tien Shan.

Heavenly mountains

The Tien Shan is a very beautiful area. In Chinese its name means "heavenly mountains." There are deep **gorges**, rushing rivers, **alpine** meadows, glaciers, and snowcapped peaks. Ibex and mountain sheep graze on high pasture, and are sometimes hunted by the rare snow leopard. Wild fruit trees, roses, and tulips grow on many of the lower slopes.

FACTS

LENGTH   1,400 miles (2,200 km)

HIGHEST POINT   Pik Pobedy, Kyrgyzstan, 24,406 feet (7,439 m)

LOCATION   Central Asia: Kyrgyzstan and Xinjiang province, China

Wandering peoples

The Chinese Uygurs and the native people of Kyrgyzstan both follow the religion of Islam. Their ancestors were **nomads** who ruled a large part of northern China many centuries ago.

Some Kyrgyz people still wander the highland areas, living in felt tents called **yurts**. But most Uygurs have settled as farmers. They are also famous for their work with silver, and make their own musical instruments to play along to their dances.

25

The New Guinea Range

The tenth longest mountain range runs down the middle of New Guinea. This mountain island is in the Pacific Ocean. Its western half, called Irian Jaya, belongs to Indonesia. The eastern half is a separate country called Papua New Guinea.

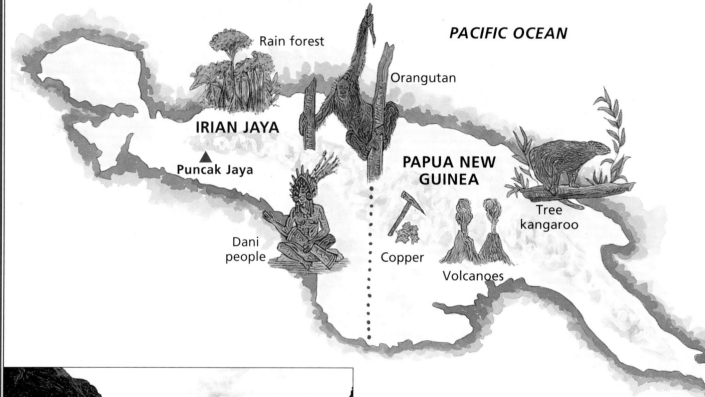

Rain forest

PACIFIC OCEAN

Orangutan

IRIAN JAYA

Puncak Jaya

PAPUA NEW GUINEA

Dani people

Copper

Volcanoes

Tree kangaroo

On the edge

Like all volcanic mountain ranges, the New Guinea range is at the edge of one of the plates that make up the Earth's crust. New Guinea is at the north end of the Indo-Australian plate, where it meets the Pacific plate. There are few active volcanoes on the island, but in 1951 a glowing cloud of gas, steam, and molten rock killed 2,000 people at the bottom of Mount Lamington.

The soil on volcanic mountain ranges is very fertile. In New Guinea, thick forests cover the mountains, and streams rush down the slopes.

Copper City

Puncak Jaya is the highest mountain between the Himalayas and the Andes. At 16,503 feet (5,030 m), it is the highest point in the New Guinea Range. The area is difficult to reach, partly because of thick tropical **rain forest** on the lower slopes. In 1936 a Dutch scientist discovered copper in the mountains. Bulldozers were flown in to build a road, and by the 1970s, thousands of tons of copper were being mined. A whole town grew up around the mine. It was named Tembagapura, or Copper City. The mine has caused many problems, including **deforestation** and **pollution**.

Although New Guinea is just south of the equator, Puncak Jaya and the island's other high mountains are capped with snow and ice all year round.

FACTS

LENGTH   1,250 miles (2,000 km)

HIGHEST POINT   Puncak Jaya, Irian Jaya, Indonesia, 16,503 feet (5,030 m)

LOCATION   New Guinea, in the Pacific Ocean

Highland villages

Many different peoples, including the Dani and the Jalé, live in the highlands of New Guinea. Their villages are far from others in the mountains, and their way of life stayed the same for many years. Now that copper and other metals have been discovered, there has been more **tourism** to parts of the world that used to be hard to reach. As a result, the lives and land of these peoples are changing.

The World's Mountain Ranges

The five longest mountain ranges in the world are on five different continents: South America, North America, Asia, Australia, and Antarctica. There are big mountain ranges on the other two continents, Europe and Africa, too.

The Alps

The Alps are the highest mountain range in Europe, although the mountain ranges in Norway and Sweden, and the Apennines in Italy are longer. The Alps stretch for more than 620 miles (1,000 km), from southeast France, across Italy, Switzerland, Germany, and Austria, to the Hungarian lowlands. Europe's highest mountain, Mont Blanc (shown right), is between France and Italy. It is 15,771 feet (4,807 m) high and has more than 20 glaciers. Many rivers and streams flow down from the glaciers. A road tunnel runs through Mont Blanc, from France to Italy.

The Ural Mountains

The northern end of the Ural Mountains is above the Arctic Circle, in north Russia. The mountain range runs north to south for 1,243 miles (2,000 km), forming the border between Europe and Asia. The highest peak is Mount Narodnaja, which is 6,217 feet (1,895 m) high. The Ural Mountains are rich in iron, nickel, copper and gold. The Ural River flows 1,575 miles (2,535 km) from the mountains to the Caspian Sea.

The Atlas Mountains

The Atlas Mountains (shown right) are a mountain chain made up of different ranges leading into each other. The chain is over 1,180 miles (1,900 km) long. It stretches from the Atlantic coast of Morocco, across northern Algeria to Tunisia and the Mediterranean Sea. In many places, the Atlas Mountains form the northern edge of the Sahara, the largest desert in the world. In spite of the heat lower down, many high Atlas Mountains are covered with snow for much of the year. This includes the highest peak, Mount Toubkal, which is 13,665 feet (4,165 m) high.

The Appalachian Mountains

The wooded hills of the Green Mountains in Vermont are part of the Appalachian Mountains. This great mountain range runs down the east coast for almost 1,243 miles (2,000 km), from Maine to Alabama.

The highest peak is Mount Mitchell, in North Carolina, which is 6,683 feet (2,037 m) high. The mountains were much higher when they formed around 300 million years ago. There are many national parks throughout the mountain range.

Glossary

Aboriginal painting in Australia

active volcano A volcano that may erupt at any time

alpine On high mountains

cannery A factory where food is put in cans

conquest Taking control by force

continent A huge area of land

crust The Earth's outer shell

deforestation Clearing land of trees

erode To wear away

erupt To throw out melted rock, ash, and steam with great force

eucalyptus A tall evergreen tree that grows in warm places

foothills The lower hills around the edge of a mountain range

generator A machine that turns one form of energy, such as the power of water, into electricity

glacier A large piece of ice that moves very slowly

gold rush Large numbers of people moving to an area where gold has been found

gorge A steep, rocky, narrow pass.

hydroelectric Making electricity using the force of moving water

ibex A wild goat with curved, ridged horns that lives in high mountain areas

ice field A huge piece of ice covering a large area of high land in the mountains

ice sheet A thick layer of ice covering a large area of land

ice shelf A huge piece of ice floating on the ocean and attached to land

Aleuts paddling a kayak

iceberg A very large piece of ice floating in the ocean

iron ore A mineral that is mined to produce iron

manganese A light gray metal that is used to make steel

mestizo A person with both European and Native American ancestors

mineral Any natural, solid material found in the Earth that does not come from plants or animals

molten Melted

nomads People who wander from place to place to find food and grazing land for their animals

outback The part of Australia that is partly covered with low plants and some trees

peak The pointed top of a mountain

peninsula A strip of land that sticks out into the ocean

plain Flat land with few trees

plate A huge piece of the Earth's outer shell

plateau A flat area of high land

pollution Damage caused by poisons

quartz A stone used to make glass and also used as jewelry

rain forest Thick forest found in warm tropical areas of heavy rainfall

salt lake A lake that often dries up in hot weather, leaving a thick layer of salt

satellite survey Measurements taken by photographing the Earth from space

Tupi natives in the Brazilian rain forest

settler A person who goes to live in a new place

snow line The place on a mountain above which there is always snow

strait A narrow body of water between two areas of land

tourism Services that help people travel for pleasure

tree line The place on a mountain above which no trees grow

tsunami A giant ocean wave caused by a volcanic eruption

tungsten A hard, gray metal

violent storm A storm that causes a lot of damage

weathering The wearing away of rocks by the weather

yurt A tent with a round top used by people in Central Asia

zinc A shiny blue-white metal used to coat iron and in electric batteries

Nomads outside their tent, in Central Asia

Index

Words in **bold** appear in the glossary on pages 30-31.

© 1996 Belitha Press Ltd.